Spiritual Friends Six

Inspirational Therapeutic Prose Poems

William Consiglio DMin

"And when at last you find someone

to whom you feel you can pour out your soul,

you stop in shock at the words you utter—

they are so rusty, so ugly, so meaningless and feeble

from being kept in the small cramped dark inside you
so long."

Sylvia Plath

Changes

My spiritual life is changing, it has become more:

Eclectic, which means my growing faith has tapped

into different thought-forms, perspectives,

and even other religious traditions.

Expansive, which means my growing faith has

broadened me to beauty and nature and

appreciation of the goodness

and kindness found in all people.

Inclusive, means that I have softened

the sharp boundaries in my thinking

about people and practices which

once I excluded and judged.

Authentic, which means I have embraced and accepted

the truth about myself,

my feelings and my life,

even if they contradict previous convictions,

which once I denied or concealed.

<u>Transparent</u> means I have become

much more willing, fearless, and confident

about revealing the truth to myself,

and about myself to others.

<u>Loving</u> means that I am allowing myself

to experience the vulnerability of

loving others, forgiving, and receiving

love more often.

<u>Devotional,</u> I have become much more

simple, less complicated or polemical;

more spontaneously childlike;

focusing on a faith of trust, hope and love

which I have for each Person of the Trinity.

We live our lives and pray our lives,

not nicely, not neatly, not often clearly or orderly,

but always authentically.

Our biography, with all its ups and downs,

is our spirituality. We have met God in our living.

There is space in God's heart for all things;

our confusion, indifference, betrayal, contradiction,

our many, many failures, and even our sin.

The trouble with my former religious thinking

is the way it complicated my life and my

relationship to God with so many peripherals,

some of which were quite attractive;

but leading me far from the essentials.

The richness of my former religious thinking

was also its most potentially misleading,

even deceiving seduction.

I ask, was Jesus eclectic, expansive,

inclusive, authentic, transparent,

loving and devotionally childlike?

"In this world let us be like Jesus."

1 John 4:17

"That the body of Christ may be built up

until we all reach unity in the faith

and in the knowledge of the Son of God,

and become mature, attaining to

the whole measure of the fullness of Christ."

Safety in the Storm

None of us has as much control

over our lives as we pretend -

a recent lesson come home to all,

to which we all must bend.

For on this April destined day

a storm with windswept pouring rain,

which any other day and time

so commonly pertained;

but not this year and not this time

when we are germbound in our home;

for with the winds and rain so fierce

a hurricane has come.

Outside there is a raging wind,

of something in the air,

an infectious death unseen,

a fear we cannot bare,

consuming every withered weed,

a pestilence concealed.

Can I be safe when thousands

fall by my side revealed?

Have we so long obeyed the ruler

of the evil powers of the air?

None can escape this airy mite,

its penetrating unseen bite.

But God shall be my refuge,

a safety in the storm;

a mighty fortress He appears,

commanding all the unseen swarm,

the noxious atmosphere.

Call Me Jesus!

For all I think I know,

I know nothing;

a heart that's lost,

something missing in me.

I am not alive, but dead inside,

waiting at Bethany

for Jesus, for Jesus,

to call me back to life.

I once lived,

but since have died,

and I stink internally.

Decades wrapped in

burial clothes,

no one to plead for me.

I plead for others

in ministry,

and no one pleads for me.

Living Love

I shall not fret about prayer ever gain,

for God has made it clear

that Churches, formulas and rituals,

methods, types and forms of prayer

are not essential at all.

What is essential is that I

should love,

for love is the highest form of prayer.

A love that passes between

me and my Father -

going one way and the other -

as a ladder between heaven and earth.

From heaven to earth,

for prayer begins with God, not me.

He offers an invitation

over and over again.

Then the love passes

so rapidly that it becomes one;

with sighs, or groans, or a gentle touch;

in warming stirrings within the heart.

This is everything and all of prayer.

Abiding always in faith and hope,

in trusting confidence and mostly love.

A childlike seeking for my Father,

already found,

and only finding him and knowing him

by endlessly seeking after him.

This is prayer!

Forget all you learned before.

There is no other more vital prayer

than this, and this is praying all day long.

The more we free ourselves from structures

and idols, and simplify our spiritual life

with childlike love of God the Father and Jesus,

the more our union with God becomes

a reality. Union is love! Love is union!

Loving communion is all the prayer

I need, and all that God desires.

LOST

What happens when a young man

takes a wrong path?

Who's to blame?

He's doing all the drugs he can get.

He says because it makes life easier.

Reality sucks. He says.

With it goes deception and lying.

He's a mystery to himself.

And now he's addicted.

He can't stop, he has to do it.

He's as lost as lost can be.

He's lost with his problems

and he's lost without them.

What went wrong inside the mind,

the heart, the soul?

I'm sorry he says again and again

to everyone.

He's disappointed everyone

and mostly himself.

O what pain love brings!

He didn't cause it,

he can't control it,

much less cure it.

Wounded, he leaves wounds for all.

The Sun-soaked Chair

Lady Robin returns this Spring

to find her nest still there;

at the top of the stairs near the back door deck

where I sit in my sun-soaked chair.

For five years now her birthing bed

lies hid within the vine;

hanging over the step where I have to pass,

she flutters and flees each time.

Now in late May, this year it was -

I spied within the nest;

two feathery fledglings having soft warm heads,

thought I was their mother's breast.

They chirped so loud, so filled with fright,

Lady bird swooped my head by.

She cackled and screeched, she fluttered and preached,

and it seemed she began to cry:

"Away! Away!", she warned me loud,

"How dare you touch my chicks.

Are you the god sitting in the sun-soaked chair

which I passed with the twigs and sticks?"

Yes, he sits there with his pen and pad,

he looks about; composes.

Then after awhile slowly in his sun-soaked chair

he drops his pen and dozes.

He's dreaming, meaning no one harm,

this old man sleeping there;

and Lady Robin glides low and high

as he sleeps in his sun-soaked chair.

Empty Church

The door unlocked, so I stepped in.

No lights were on, the place was dim.

Into an empty church today,

I took some time to think and pray.

The windows had been closed so long,

for such a lengthy time;

so stuffiness had filled the place

with the airless quarantine.

And yet there was a presence

of the people who worshiped there;

for I saw where each one sat each week

as if they were still here.

No hymns I heard, no organ played,

no words were spoken out;

yet I could hear the preacher

and the reader still about.

I knelt upon the cushions

that circled the altar rail;

I raised my eyes to the wooden cross

from years so worn and pale.

It was not long when then I thought

I heard the chapel door;

it creaked and seemed to open wide;

were footsteps on the floor?

Was I alone? Who had come in?

I dared not look to see.

I wondered who had joined me in

the dim lit sanctu'ry.

I hoped the one had worn a mask;

would keep six feet away.

I guess I was annoyed by this,

I came to pray alone today.

I tried to close my eyes once more,

I bowed my troubled head;

that's when I heard a voice within,

and this is what it said:

"No virus, no pandemic,

no world predicament,

has made me turn away from those

who each week are participants

in this my house, my temple true;

for those who come within.

Nothing can take you from my care,

no sickness, faults or sin.

I Am your Father God,

your Jesus is my Son,

in you the Holy Spirit dwells,

we there with you are One.

I know he's washing me!

God is washing out this world,

I'm sure that's what I see;

His hand is moving through the earth,

I know he's washing me.

He's cleaning every river,

every city, sewer and town;

he's cleaning out each one of us,

our greed is coming down.

Yes, God is washing out his world!

He's walking through the meadows,

o'er hills and mountain heights,

and everywhere he steps his foot

comes something pure and bright.

Bringing down the arrogant,

the scoffers and the guile;

lifting up the pure of heart,

shutting out the vile.

Yes, God is washing out his world!

What's dark is turning whiter,

what's red, a deeper red;

the hidden sins and secrets

are all exposed instead.

Country after nation,

creeds of every kind;

people rich and peasant poor,

no one is left behind.

God is washing out his world,

I'm sure that's what I see;

His hand is moving o'er the globe,

I know he's washing me,

O Yes,

I know he's washing me!

God Experiences Me

I don't experience God!

God experiences me!

There are thoughts and feelings

within me that are too difficult

and too nuanced for which to find words.

They are at best, deep murmurs.

They are very real experiences,

but they are inexpressible.

One is loneliness,

or loneliness whenever I experience God,

or God experiences me.

He makes me very lonely.

When he reveals his depths before me,

often in a split second,

when he shows me himself,

it is intolerable, frightening, lonely,

and sad.

I fall into a bottomless well of being alone there,

even if I have many close people beside me.

It's the loneliness of death.

For to know God is to die; to myself.

No one can enter into my death experience with me.

No one but my Father God and Jesus.

It's the loneliness of death,

in which no other person,

no matter how much I know of their love for me,

can share with me.

For death is more than we can bear,

and it is ours alone.

It stirs the depths of loneliness, fear and loss.

Who can survive the experience of dying?

Yet we survive; we arrive, alive!

Dying is what I should have been doing,

or was doing, all my life.

Passing over through Jesus to the Father.

If I let my loneliness be felt;

if I hold onto it for awhile,

rather than run from it,

I enter most fully into the mystery of my being;

the mystery of human emptiness,

and absolute solitude;

my non-existence and nothingness.

Nothing but the ethereal spirit.

And there as spirit I join with

the Holiest Spirit,

and loneliness ends,

for I emerge with my true identity,

a child of God;

and God experiences me as his own

at last.

I'm loved

I'm the peanut in your butter,

I'm the jelly in your donuts,

I'm the numbers on your clock,

and the leaves upon your plant.

When you love me I'm elated,

when you care for me I'm thrilled.

When I feel loved, I feel so free,

I feel liberated and accepted

even in my ugly nakedness.

I know I'm loved because

I'm part of the universe,

I am a gift to be here.

I belong, I'm included,

I feel understood and can

relax like an unprotected kitten

curled up in the summer sun.

BLESSED TRINITY

O Holy Three,

I bow my head before,

to worship and adore.

O Holy Mystery,

with understanding low,

my love I come to show.

O Holy Spirit.

change me through,

and all within renew.

O Jesus Lord,

heal this battered heart,

from me ne'er depart.

O Abba Father,

turn my life around,

make me whole and sound.

Let it be! Amen!

I Did!

The Father, softly to my heart,

Spoke that I His love to you impart;

That I should pray this day for you,

And so I did, and will, and do!

Bill 828

Waiting

What am I waiting for?

It feels like I'm waiting more.

Can't go on with my life none

until this waiting is done.

But my life *is* going on,

stop waiting for this virus end.

Stop waiting for a vaccine cure,

when you're certain all is sure.

There's no wait for springtime flowers,

nor groundhogs, birds or deer,

who live within my land about;

they have come out this year.

I even saw a bobcat stroll

not more than ten yards by;

I nearly fell from off my chair,

he looked so feral sly.

The sober season Lent has gone,

and so has Easter time;

the holy journey of the Church

delays not bell or chime.

Get on with living here and now;

plant some seeds, expect to sow.

Write some lyrics, sing a song,

be yourself, wait not long

to feed your eyes upon the green,

end longing for what had been.

Catch up with God, He's movin' on,

He doesn't live with what has gone.

Whatever is, that's where He'll be,

with eyes on Him, you're sure to see

that what you're waiting for,

is here, is now, outside your door.

Crossroad

The silence of a wounded world

appears for me at dusk each eve,

when traffic on the streets is low

and people snuggle close to home

where safely fam'lies cleave.

A silence falls like from the sky

upon the children in their beds

whom all day long have been denied

their parents honest dread.

Then sit they at the kitchen table

before a dim lit lamp,

and dare to glance if they are able

upon their faces anxious stamped.

Expenses owed and he's no work,

time's weight hangs o're their heads,

as dark clouds shadow and disturb,

and rain once pleasant on the roof,

now threatens them instead.

Where once there was a freedom

to hug and touch and speak;

even more they know they need 'em,

in a world that can seem bleak.

We're born and live awhile it seems

to farm or fish or sow our field;

then quickly old, with sickly dreams,

we wonder what our life has yield.

So fast do people come and go,

we know that's our fate too.

Life, which like a passing show,

unlasting and with nothing new.

This is a crossroad for the globe,

for insecure, unsafe and weak,

all children hence will surely probe,

when eve'ning brings disturbing sleep.

Yet Father, hallowed, we say still;

there is yet faith upon this earth.

Your kingdom come, be done your will,

please grant us all a holy birth!

Mr Jay

I wandered through the countryside

to find a place to pray;

with ardent thirst I sought the Lord,

pursuing him all day.

Then came upon a hillside church

I almost passed about.

Twenty people gather there;

no more I surely doubt.

I looked and then I pondered

if my Lord is present there.

They call themselves a house of God;

was this an answer to my prayer?

The leader was a bearded man

with a wife and children two.

I wonder what support he gets;

how much could each one show!

A Mr Jay was there that day;

he saw the women wear,

a lacy covering o're their heads,

and men with flowing hair.

Everyone was dressed in black;

their God he guessed was grave.

They never laugh or speak out loud,

nor children misbehave.

The ladies all must sit alone,

and so the men do too.

The women's dress was hot and dark

and blacker were their shoes.

The preaching was a long affair,

an hour or even two;

and the burden of his fiery words

was not that God loves you.

He gravely spoke about the law

and how it must be kept;

then Mr Jay spoke out at last

and asked which law is best.

The leader and the people

turned with shocked dismay,

for no one ev'r inquired like this;

no one up to this day.

The preacher stunned and stammered

that all the law is one,

and we must keep the greatest

and smallest; everyone!

Then Mr Jay quote loud and clear,

to love our God wholly;

with all our heart and soul and strength,

from Deuteronomy.

He also said that each of us

must dearly love another;

the poor, despised and enemy

as if they were our brother.

The twenty murmured with delight,

this was so new to hear.

To love like we are loved

with mercy, kindness, care.

This was a different God

which Mr Jay proclaimed.

They asked that he would tell them more,

but this is how he explained.

He called upon a crippled man

and asked what is the best;

to keep the Sabbath law

or to be healed and blest.

The law of love and mercy

always comes first of all;

and touching him upon his legs,

the man rose strong and tall.

When Mr Jay left church that day,

the twenty followed J.

It was his God whom they had found

whom they would love always.

Silent Church

Once inside the empty church

again I went to pray.

I passed the sweet mown grass

and the iris on the way.

I opened wide the creaking door

and paused in the entryway;

a dry and airless atmosphere;

so one brief moment stayed.

Within the darkened chapel

I turned on lights to see;

then walked up to the kneeling place

to seek Him longingly.

I vowed that I would stay this time

as long as it might take,

until I heard the Father's voice

and I to Him awake.

I knelt upon the cushion

with arms upon the wood;

then bowed my head and closed my eyes,

and waited best I could.

At first the sounds around came forth,

my mind preoccupied.

The cracking roof, expanding pews,

the murmur of the cars gone by.

Then suddenly no sounds at all,

completely silent, still.

I spoke my name and then these words,

"In me your word fulfill".

"You know me, all about me,

my past and present too.

You know my heart's sincerity,

what's old and what is new.

There's nothing now for me to hide,

You've known me at my worst;

so I will truthful, honest be,

You know for You I thirst.

I lay myself before you

as candid as can be;

I wait to hear what you will say

most Holy Trinity."

Nothing then but silence,

no word or thought He spoke;

until I deeper sought Him,

and I more fully woke.

The words He spoke for me to pray,

which He desired from me.

"I love you Father, Jesus, Spirit,

with love entirely."

No more was felt than that of love,

just silent heartfelt love.

No other thoughts or words or prayers

were prayed this day above.

Sun Rise

I rose before the new day's dawning

to see the sun arise.

The sky, painted yellow-red,

spilled into my eyes.

A flaming fan of shooting shafts

pierced the blanket blue;

a fierce bright eye of circled gold

broke through.

The distant hills smiled with delight

and the birds more boldly sang;

the sky now striped with spectrum rays

of orange color sprang.

O Sun! Warm like the mother-womb,

secure in Your firmament

which our body ne'er forgets,

resorts to Your permanence .

O Sun! You warm my furrowed face,

and wrap me in Your awful bright,

as on that day of days when first was spoke

"Let there be Light!"

Never Cease Appealing

How feeble my faith

when on the earth

a pestilence so concealing,

makes cries ring out,

"Protect good Lord

from fears that I am feeling."

How trust is tried,

surrenders not

wholly to Him in yielding,

but draws within its

turtle shell,

protects its once believing.

How hope's delayed;

weak, afraid,

to exert its once idealing,

when all about

there is a shout

how scant the word of healing.

How former strong

with prayers so long

upon my knees was kneeling,

but now my faith

seems to abate,

its weakness is revealing.

How low I've shown

myself I've known,

but there is yet a ceiling;

for I am awed

before my God,

and never cease appealing.

story of my life

The story of my life:

died peacefully at 83,

no, let's make it 88.

in torment many days

all my life

unhealthy of mind

a marriage of a kind

all marriages differ

what's better or for worse

better for me

worse for her

but she's strong

i am weak and wounded more.

self-indulgent

selfish

a tyrant perhaps

distancing others

causing pain

even more selfish

self-preoccupied

self-protecting

she is generous

persevering

honest to a fault

careful

pains-taking

careful

right is right

creates beauty

loves the land

wounded also

i am talented

but so is she

i'm artistic

creative

passionate

cooks, sings, writes

teaches

paints

preaches

poet

but wounded also

predominantly wounded.

daughters

night and day

shades of gray

one like mother

one like father.

so alone

am i

really lonely

college teacher

27 years

retired,

teacher

counselor

minister

students, clients pleasing

mask to hide

torment below

graduate school.

seminary

seminal hiding

God

religion

oppressed

obsessed

impressed.

high school

distant close

teacher

emotionally dependent

sad at his death

glee club

love boy crush

sad at his death

oddball

oddball teachers.

grade school

troubled already shows

mister smith principal

basketball score keeper

locker room fear

failure, failure

anxiety

fear of aggression

mister oneto baseball

humiliation

skeeter

misfit.

family

italian

intense

frightening

disturbing

attached

disturbed

eroticise

exposed

different one

lost, lonely

indulgent

attached

cried

howled

bawled

born.

Poem 400

Napping.

I meet her in the cafeteria

provided for the faculty

she is sitting alone

with a cup of coffee

I can't see her face

but I know she's black

and so is the coffee

in a cream cup and saucer.

She has strange teeth

she's not pretty

and she knows it

so she welcomes company.

She is the only black person

I've really known

I sit with her at the table

she smiles

she doesn't have many friends

she's new.

She has a problem with drinking

calls me some nights drunk

I never tell her when she's sober

I don't know how to ask her

she wouldn't remember

that she was lonely and afraid

anyways, just like me.

what's *my* addiction?

She spills her coffee

I go get her another cup

very graciously

when I return

I'm not sure she's there.

But it happens again

something's wrong with me

I'm on the floor and can't get up

nobody's around to help me

I feel alone and stupid

no one knows me like this

lonely, helpless and stupid.

Is she dead or alive

I wonder

it's been many years.

Why am I thinking of her today?

Is she thinking of me?

Is Jack dead or alive?

Is he thinking of me somewhere?

Poor sad gay Jack

maybe one of these.

Never heard from her since

my farcical retirement dinner.

It's Trinity Sunday today

thirty-four years later

imagine that.

I'll visit the Empty Church

like the Church itself.

That was a potshot.

I'll think about the Trinity.

Once I had it all figured out.

But this is a milestone day

at least for me

my four hundredth poem.

It only matters to me.

(Living with regret

shame, shame.

Shame is disappointment

with myself

in myself for who I am).

I can't get up

I'm helpless

hopeless?

Now I'm anxious

my legs are weak.

My legs struggle and scuffle

I must awake

from the sofa where I nap

with the red velvet coverall.

I hear a woodpecker nearby

tapping some tree

and the clock is ticking

tapping the air

shadows across the lawn

move in the breeze

a bright sunny day

it's June 7, 2020

my four hundredth poem.

I tossed my computer

I tossed my computer out the window

two stories, no,

make that five stories down.

A life's work destroyed.

Free at last.

But now I'm lost

all my attachments gone.

I cried, regretted, got angry.

Tried piecing it together,

Tried to reassemble it.

Why did I?

The way to God

is computerless.

God will never appear on a screen,

nor can the www reveal Him

No JC with a PC.

Can I have one with the other?

He's calling even as I write.

I hear His faint voice

like a warm heart-touch.

I'd rather hear and see nothing

than always something

that means nothing.

Eyes always watching

earphones always hearing

so I never hear the Spirit

whispering in my spirit-heart

my life is too noisy

searching for pretty thoughts

or feelings, or to make

something happen.

Can't tolerate silent stillness.

Go into your inner room

close the door

speak to your Father.

He can't be conjured up

just evoking my own version

of Him and never knowing

the real One.

Leave him alone.

Stop searching

and he'll find me

and show Himself real.

All these many months

I've been apart from Him.

He was taking me deeper

into a cave.

I dive into the deep end

where there is no water

into nothing

only to be held

and float in nothing.

How can I live this way?

Ah, but,

the sound of Nothing's voice

saying nothing

is everything.

Poeming is

As long as I live

and have health

I'll be poeming.

Poems are sugar, salt,

spice, medicine, balm.

Without them I shrivel up

and die.

Feelings and words get stuck

inside my throat.

I need to talk and tell.

Poems are life-savers

on this ship.

Every time I get tossed

into the surging sea

poems float out to save me.

The other day I walked

in the new mown grass

among the living dead

and saw my tombstone.

I was not there,

just leftover bones

covered with soil.

A six foot skeleton

resting in the ground.

I miss them

but I'm not there.

Can't wait till I join them again.

But I live

because he lives

and lived in me

and lives in me and I in Him.

There were dead dead

and living dead.

Dead without Him

dead with Him.

He is Life.

Whoever believes in the Son

has eternal life already.

He gave me poeming

for my therapy

and spirituality,

breathing

words of life.

The Word is Life.

Proeming,

prosaic poetry.

Poems lie all about the tomb

Read them!

Listen to your life!

Crooked

I came upon a crooked tree

near the path within the wood.

For years it grew this way and that,

then straight the way it should.

A crooked woman came in his sight

on a Sabbath long ago;

bent for eighteen years was she,

her spine was like a bow.

That day he placed his hand on her;

she rose up strong and straight;

she shouted glory, glory to God,

after ten long years and eight.

But on that day the leader said,

"You scorn the Sabbath law,

for on this day no work is done,"

but others looked with awe.

Jesus looked upon this chief

and asked him most direct,

"Is not to heal on any day,

God's work of kind respect?"

"This woman's crooked spine

was healed by God through me;

is this then not enough for you

to understand and see?"

O Jesus Christ my Savior,

how blind that I can't see,

for you have healed my crookedness,

and now have set me free.

(Luke 13:10-17)

POEM

May the grace of the Lord Jesus Christ,

and the love of God the Father,

and the fellowship of the Holy Spirit

be with you all.

My Father loves me everlastingly,

it never goes away;

grows deeper, stronger, staggering,

with every passing day.

His loves bows down to lift me up,

His hand rests on my head.

He whispers love within my soul,

while by his hand I'm led.

I stumble, trip and fall so oft'

in this life's perilous way.

Yet He cares for me and loves me;

provides, protects, each day.

He forgives and takes me back

when I have failed and sinned.

He comforts and He blesses me;

He touches me within.

O Father, how I thank you

for all you've done for me.

Please draw me even closer

and set my whole life free.

Like a Tree

A tiny seed falls into the lap

of Mother Earth, and resting

its head on her warm bosom, goes asleep.

When it wakes, the miracle of life

has begun where the moist soil

and warm sunlight keep.

It feels and finds what it needs

with infallible instinct,

gathering food from the soil that's nigh,

and strength from the rocks

on which it wraps its first tender roots

and drinks from the nearby stream and sky.

It imprisons the sunlight deep within

until its garments are a living green.

It bows to the winds and bends

to the storms and blushes

under the warm gaze of the ardent sun

until it's strong and straight, rising above

the other trees where once unseen.

Tall it grows with lusty stretches,

spreading its branches over the earth

and lifting its head to salute the heavens.

Then quickly birds appraise its concealing

caverns to build their nests within its boughs.

"Whosoever will may come," the tree

proclaims its gospel in their presence.

Now the humble beasts from the fields,

the cattle and the sheep, and weary men

come to rest in its shade and at its feet;

and when its fruit grows to luscious ripeness

she says, "Take and eat!"

If you will not come and take from

my branches in the late summer and

autumn ripeness, then I will drop deserving

fruit into your lap or give generously to

the squirrels, birds and beasts,

for I was conceived to serve.

I, by the grace of God have survived,

baring my head to the titanic tempests,

my face exposed to the snow and ice;

attacked by the storms and the stresses

of young men's knives carving

their ardor into my skin.

Worse is the woodsman assaulting me

with the sharp edge of his ax striking

close to my heart, and I must yield

with sap-flows of tears to feed the fires

and proudly warm his home as he desires.

Now is seen the record of my years,

the good and bad, the rot and ruin

of disease and plague attacks.

I draw a circle around my heart

of each passing year of all that's

said and thought with facts.

I have survived many generations

who make me their friend.

The children of the children have sat below,

overhearing their sorrows and their joys.

Sometimes I listen and laugh or weep.

Sweethearts have uttered the same

sentiments for five hundred years

and I their secrets keep.

A dying soldier of domestic wars

in blue and gray and bloody red

gave forth his last breath in my arms.

Bullets and bombs have struck me sorely

yet I stand strong to comfort

the weary workmen from their farms.

Personal pilgrimages return to me

to celebrate a time of bliss.

They listen, for trees do speak,

leaning on my solid side and picking pieces

for souvenirs. I tell them of days gone by

when they were young with hopes, and meek.

God takes a thousand years to grow a tree,

and in one brief hour man cuts down

my years of determined heroic growth.

What wanton desecration to kill a tree.

Thank God for trees!

I would hate to live where there are none.

"I think that I shall never see

a poem as lovely as a tree.

Poems are made like fools like me,

but only God can make a tree."

Wonderful as is a tree,

more wonderful a living soul

as in this primary psalm, as told:

"He shall be like a tree,

planted by streams of water."

He trusts that rain will come as needed,

that sunshine penetrate it deeply,

and soil will nurture her completely.

Such a tree is full of prayer

for prayer is merely trust;

she knows all things together work

if loving God she must.

O suffering she must endure

for suffering is part of growth,

of this she is most sure.

"He shall be like a tree

which yields its fruit in season,

whose leaf does not wither -

whatever he does prospers."

(from God's Open, 1924)

Whom the Lord loves

You say you're loved by God.

Prove it!

How do you know?

You'll be chastened,

that's how it shows.

I've been chastised,

disciplined, reproved,

and corrected more than once.

It hurt, still hurts; it cost.

He did it; my Father,

because he loves me

and would not see me lost.

You think he's gonna

let the devil, this evil world

or your flesh have you?

No way!

No! He's gonna strip you

of what you cherish,

of that sin that draws you away.

He's gonna break your heart,

for a while,

till your heart is his again.

Till it breaks for Him.

Go ahead Lord! Do it Lord!

Break me till tears run pain.

Yes, you love me,

but I fear your love;

it's fire, it's power,

it smarts, and awe-filled.

You're a fierce Lover;

Jealous, Zealous, and law-filled.

Remember

Shadrach, Meshach,

Abednego?

And that fourth person,

the Angel of the Lord,

O blessed Jesus,

walking about in the furnace

of my life.

Your fires will not harm me

because you're gonna be

with me, this I know.

Go ahead!

Withdraw from me

till I beg you return.

Or I'll just weep and weep

and miss you something awful.

Hold me by your heart

When have I just given You

thanks and praise

because you are who you are.

Who you are: that's the problem.

You have become more distant,

elusive and uncertain now.

That's the way it should be.

Outgrow your Jesus pictures

and bearded Father images,

all anthropomorphics;

your warm feelings and bright insights.

I want You Yourself more now

and can't see or touch you.

Can't hold onto you,

I am approaching the real.

Can only grasp and have you by faith.

The assurance of things unseen,

confidence in what is hoped for,

seeing in the dark.

Your nature God, is the very essence

of my being, as a tree is to an apple.

You are the center of my self.

Your red fire courses through my veins.

You are my life.

Without you I would not exist, and

I cannot cease to exist because of You.

I am created in your image.

I am spirit as You are Spirit.

You absorb me completely.

The juice of my peach,

the pit of my plum.

There is no separating from you.

You are my Self,

my inner being, my spirit.

I must "practice your presence"

and live from the center of my being.

Not the circumference of life,

but to live from You,

the stationary center of the wheel

which goes round and round.

"The secret place of the Most High"

and the treasure hidden in my heart.

I must practice the stillness,

the solitude, and the silence

to be with You. To be!

I live by faith and not by sight.

By the faith of the Son of God.

Faith like water

escaping from my hand

and draining in the sand.

Like the Evening Primrose,

the Scarlet Pimpernel,

glowing when it's dark,

gone by light.

Like the wind, inhaled breath

then exhaled, You live in me.

I know it's you, but there's

nothing to grasp.

More and more I must live

in the spirit and truth where you are

who is Spirit most Holy.

Father-love has been poured into our hearts

through the Holy Spirit who has been given to us.

We know we are your children

for you have given us your Spirit

who testifies to our hearts

in subtle words and proven ways.

"Hold me by your love-experience of me!

By my care, my love,

my goodness, provision and protection.

Especially my preservation of you

through the self-made disasters of your life;

My little and big miracles.

Know me by your heart which

loves to call me Abba."

O Summer, how I love Thee

O Summer, how I love Thee!

For the freedom that you give

To roam in fields and wooded groves;

A pleasant life to live.

The sweet mown grass

And the sassafras, near the twining honeysuck vine.

When Your bright light warms the hills at morn

Where the blue-trumpet morning-glory twine.

Then You send forth the songs of the air

And the bliss of the birds which you bless.

The twitter and chirp from the trees

with its soft-honeyed tenderness.

You set clouds like pillows of white

Stitched on a canvas of blue.

Geraniums red, geraniums pink,

Neath the birdbath so solid and true.

O Summer, Who has made Thee?

Who could have authored Your Sun?

Only He that's more brilliant than Thee,

The brighter bright glorious One.

SIMPLE PRAYER

Growth in prayer

is growth in intimacy with God

and is growth in greater silence.

Doing nothing but being present

and waiting on Him. This is

a step toward intimacy with the Silent One.

But difficult for most.

It is silent loving communion with Him.

"Cor ad cor loquitor,"

Each heart speaking love to the Other.

Wordless, thoughtless communion.

Receptivity not activity.

An act of love and surrender.

Love is always allowing

oneself to be loved.

Unless we learn to receive

we cannot give love.

Letting myself be shaped

by the hands of the divine potter

on the spinning wheel of life.

It is He who initiates all true prayer.

But God does not call it prayer.

From "precari" to ask, entreat.

He does not name it at all.

He simply loves to be with you;

that is enough for Him.

Unless I allow Him to change me,

I am not allowing in His love.

Of course I will change,

as the wind changes direction

when it encounters the rock.

I must stop trying to control,

trivialize or pigeonhole God.

Let me trustingly free-fall into

His arms. This is my true

relationship to Him; to the Three.

This is simple prayer.

Become simple; a simplicity;

burn your notes on prayer

and leave it to Him.

Let Him teach you His ways.

Personal, intuitive, receptive,

contemplative, empty.

I've stopped praying altogether.

I do not pray anymore.

If I pray, I pray His prayers.

I only dwell, abide with Them.

Any healing I may do is His.

Any miracles I may do are His.

Let Them love me as They will.

"You have not chosen me,

I have chosen you!"

No longer visual or auditory,

but intuitive and simple.

Because we are the Father's children,

He has given us the Spirit of His Son within us.

And Christ's Spirit cries, "Abba, Abba!"

Can you hear Him calling to His Father,

and you with him call also?

Together you cry "Abba, Father!"

with tears and weeping

of both sadness and joy.

Sadness because so few know Abba.

Joy because you are not worthy

that He knows and loves you.

If I stop grasping for Him

He takes hold of me.

He finds me in every condition

and loves me - when I'm broken, bruised,

bleeding, out of sorts, out of my mind,

distant, indifferent, and apathetic.

When I let others down;

when I let myself down.

When I'm filled with regret or shame.

When others have rejected me,

He has received me home

with a robe, and fine sandals,

and an intimate feast for four.

My Little Church

Ah! my own little church!

A place quite plain and simple.

A steepled roof, no bigger

than a humble farmyard stable.

See the church that's nestled there -

a chapel made of stone;

just tucked away beside a brook

in a hollow all alone.

A simple cross hangs on the wall,

above two candles where

our eyes are drawn in reverence,

to Christ who's honored here.

No need for a cathedral,

pipe organs swelling grand;

the organ in my little church

in a corner does it stand.

Don't need complex creeds

or repetitious words;

instead we need a loving touch

which vital faith preserves.

No more than fifty people

gather there to pray

and worship God the Father

in the truth and Spirit way.

We sing with great devotion,

we hear the scriptures read;

then silently we listen

while we share the wine and bread.

The Father's name is lifted

and love for Jesus rings

throughout my little church,

the Spirit's joy it brings.

The preaching from the heart

imparts the Spirit's life;

it lifts the weak and weary,

makes burdens all seem light.

It tells the Father's love for us

when we had gone astray,

and how he sent his only Son

to lead us to the way.

The way back to the Father

whose children we've become;

who leaves the ninety-nine,

to find that one lost one.

Love came down to draw us up,

to show our waywardness;

God was Love in Jesus Christ

who met us at the cross.

My little church brings love to all,

the poor, the sick, the dying;

the hungry, lost, bereaving ones,

the furrowed tears from crying.

O come and let Him bless you

in our chapel made of stone;

the little church beside the brook,

you'll never be alone.

Breathe along with Thee

Ah! How I love You Silent One.

Your silence so intense,

so filling, near,

so present that

I cannot move when You are here.

A Frozen euphoria.

A Seduced surrender.

Only stillness and adore.

Everywhere like the air,

follows after everyone.

Breathing Spirit on us

and igniting hearts

whosoever will.

You consume us like fire

and we burn.

O what love;

what forgiving sacrificial love

You the Silent One offers me;

yet Your face I cannot see.

Your silence speaks a million words

though I in perfect rest

lean upon Your breast

and hear your Spirit-heart

and breathe along with Thee.

Each breath Your presence tells,

like soundless convent bells

toll love for me.

Each silent touch reveals

a deep-like well profound

that all my life assembles

in an instant, flashing before me,

as at the moment of death,

dying to see Thee.

SEERS

Seers

who receive visions,

peering into the other world

of Jesus or Mary.

Not the Father or Holy Spirit.

How wonderful to cross that border

and know with certainty who is there,

to greet me,

where you shall be also.

How mind-arresting is this.

Seeing one from the other world,

the supernatural;

incomprehensible,

but so inspiring.

The border line fades

and you slip through.

Though I want to doubt,

I also want to believe even more.

For they are either

frauds, deceived and deranged,

or so very authentic.

I have considered all.

If authentic and genuine,

then how do they see?

They are not seeing with their eyes,

though they sometimes do.

More often they are hearing

words spoken visually within,

repeating messages for all to hear.

Like prophets of old.

Like you and me at times.

From heaven, to the receptor,

becoming the transmitter.

The seer cannot be used of God

except when he faces the acrid truth

about himself and is painfully humbled,

then turns to God in extremis.

My vision was likewise.

In the midst of this poem I slept.

I saw a dream screen.

I am accused,

convicted that my whole life's a lie.

I did not live authentically.

I hid and created a false self.

Angry tears, sorrow-pain, pleading, despairing,

and knowing suicide is near

when I faced my real self and know

there is no escape for me.

Bottom falling out and no top.

They found me out and outed me.

Now I know why some suicide.

Who can I turn to?

Now I know the meaning of salvation.

Now I know a Savior.

Thanks be to the Father,

who delivers me through Jesus Christ our Lord!

Only He understands and forgives.

Only He can show me all that is lovable in me

and heal my shame and guilt.

He alone from the other side

says, "All is well. I love you. Come!"

And His arms open wide.

Breakthroughs

You hound me so!

Leave me alone!

Stop chasing after me!

Cleave me alone!

It's taken me this whole life

to realize I need another whole life

to explore and do all that

I discovered in this life.

I was just getting started

when I turned eighty.

.

"I can never read all the books I want;

I can never be all the people I want and live all the lives I want.

I can never train myself in all the skills I want.

And why do I want?

I want to live and feel all the shades, tones and variations

of mental and physical experience possible in my life.

And I am horribly limited."
—Sylvia Plath

Father you're so good to me,

you come when I don't call.

You know before I even know

what is needed most of all.

I thank you for the answers

to my many unspoken prayers.

I thank you most for being You,

my Abba Father cares.

'O Marenariello

The Young Sailor

Just sentimental Italian songs

I lova to sing alonga.

Vicin' ô mare
Facimmo 'ammore,
A core a core
Pe' nce spassà.

Sò marenaro
E tiro 'a rezza;
Ma p'allerezza
Stong'a murì.

Beside the sea
We'll make love,
Side by side
To have a good time.

I'm a sailor
And I take out the net,
But from the gladness
I'm ready to die.

Piscatore e Pusilleco

Fisherman from Pusilleco

Dorme 'o mare. Voca, voca!
Tutt'è pace attuorno a mme.
Ma pecché?
Ma pecché m'hê lassato,
Mentr'io moro stanotte pe' te?

The sea is sleeping. Row, row!
Everything is peaceful around me.
But why?
But why have you left me
While I'm dying tonight because of you?

Rusella e Maggia

Rusella e maggio mia

rusella e maggio

Tu si caduta a cielo ncopp'a sta loggia

Te vas 'nfrnta 'o sole cu 'o melio raggio

Rusiella e maggio mia

rusella e maggio.

My Rosette, of May
Rosette,
You fell from heaven on this lodge.
The sun with the best ray kisses your forehead,
Rosetta of May,
Rosetta of May

My Emmaus

We recognized him not

when he walked with us today,

but our hearts burned deep within

as we led him on the way

to Emmaus, as dusk descended,

our heads bent down in grief,

our hearts filled full of loss,

for which was no relief.

I wept when he inquired

what happened just ago.

I asked with unbelief,

"do you alone not know?"

"He is dead," I said, "the one we loved,

the Messiah thought he be.

He died by crucifixion

on a blood-stained cypress tree.

Then our hearts burned like fire

as he opened all God's Word,

and told us how the Christ

must suffer in this evil world.

Who was this man, this rabbi,

who spoke so knowingly?

He made it clear the prophets told

the Christ would die most willingly.

We listened as his piercing light

enlightened both our minds;

his voice enraptured us with love,

his spirit drove through us like winds.

As eve came on we asked him stay

and dine with us awhile.

He took some bread and blessed it,

broke and gave it with a smile.

With the taste of him within us,

and our eyes so deeply closed,

when we awoke, we knew for sure

that Jesus had arose.

That's when our eyes were opened,

and we knew this was the Lord.

When he said "Take and Eat!"

We took him at his word."

O Lord, you're with us ever

in your body and your blood;

and we are full assurance giv'n

of your closeness by your love.

Luke 24:13-35

Invocabit Me

Psalm 91:15-16

He shall cry to me, and I will hear him:

I will deliver him, and I will glorify him:

I will fill him with length of days.

He that dwells in the care of the Most High

shall abide under the protection of the God of Heaven.

Glory be to the Father, and to the Son,

and to the Holy Ghost;

as it was in the beginning,

is now, and ever shall be, world without end.

Amen

When is the last time you have

actually cried out to God the Father

or Jesus? The word "cry" above

is the Latin word "invocabit".

The Hebrew word "qara".

It can mean to "call", "cry" or even to "scream".

When you cry out most sincerely

the Father will do four things:

I will hear him. God hears us because

God is a living Person who loves us.

I will answer him. God is responsive to us.

He desires to help us and care for us.

I will deliver him. The Father provides, protects,

and preserves us continually.

I will fill him with length of days.

Our Father gives us just the amount of time

we need to acquire an intimate

relationship to Himself.

Ethan

I know a young Amish family

who have left their ancestral ways.

Husband Ethan has broken from the Amish tradition

and gone back to the Bible days,

like Luther who left the Catholic tradition before him.

Like people in churches do, year after year

questioning their once cherished customs.

Tradition verses scripture.

External religion verses interior spirituality.

Now I'm no longer fearful of death, says Ethan,

because God lives in me:

I no longer have to follow laws,

only the Spirit within.

Reminiscent of Saint Paul.

The smallest breach in the wall caused

the whole edifice to collapse for Ethan.

A small disagreement with his elders.

Though Ethan maintains some former traditions,

he has led his family to the approval

of many modern conveniences

which were once forbidden.

Tractor, car, telephone, electricity.

No more horse and buggy,

which no one will buy since he is outcast.

His family and friends have shunned him.

Even parents, the grandparents of his children:

What religion does to some!

Now his oldest daughter has leukemia.

Ethan wonders if this is God's punishment.

I know that God has healed her, Ethan says,

but the state compels him to seek medical treatment.

She is in remission now. He guesses God still cares,

and he was right after all:

His docile wife and children comply completely

because father knows best, so the Bible says.

Ethan has big signs on his car that read

"Are you sure you're going to heaven?"

He hands out tracks at the county fair

warning people about hell:

He's struggles with common sense verses the Bible.

His wife is intelligent but leaves moral matters

to her husband. Her salvation

is in caring for her house and children.

I ask you: when is religious freedom harmful?

Ethan takes his four children into the barn,

they are ten, seven, five and four.

He cuts off a chicken's head while his children

watch with wide uncertain eyes and breathless fright,

as he lectures them about "the life is in the blood",

Christ shed his blood, and gave his life.

For what? Why? What difference does it make?

the children ask as they get older.

In later years Ethan himself abandons

his strict biblical view:

He and his wife become avid consumers

at Walmart twice a week.

How fragile and precarious

and sometimes very strange

are the traditions religious people hold so firmly,

only to be dismissed quickly for simple,

practical or personal reasons.

It causes one to question

the religious conventionality under which we live.

How should we then live?

What meaning has life?

Ethan now asks.

It's been a long time since he has had

a long beard and suspenders:

His father died, so Ethan and his wife

go back for the Amish funeral.

They are received coldly,

a few are more friendly.

So many ways people have devised

to include God in their lives

and exclude others.

Convicted!

He stands before the Judge

accused of being

Insane! Not well!

From *in* = "not" + "*sanus*" = well.

It's really a benevolent word

when you understand it's truth.

Not a harsh label

but a word of sympathy.

He's pretty sure that

there's something mentally unwell

within.

It's nothing to be ashamed of;

it just simply is.

He talks out loud to a

voice of shame or blame he hears inside.

Not often but sometimes.

Usually regretting

something that happened

for which he is ashamed

or embarrassed.

So he speaks some rejection

or suppression to it

right out loud.

Like "No!" or "Nevermind!"

Usually no one else hears.

But that's not all.

He gets paranoid too,

attributing malicious motives

to people sometimes,

creating scenarios

in which he's the victim

or target of some plot.

He heard this kind of thinking

in his family

when he was growing up,

never thinking he would be like this.

But families seep in like prejudice.

He has a prejudice toward

three unnamed groups in particular.

It's too demeaning because he knows better.

Prejudice is a form of learning.

Now he wonders if as he gets older

he will slip into some kind of dementia

and this dark side

will come out uncontrollably.

He also has PTSD!

He had it most of his life,

traumatized as a child,

causing anxiety.

He has a serious case of

emotional detachment, big time.

Can't give himself to another.

Afraid of intimacy.

It's unsafe! Protection from hurt.

Messed up love.

Also a bit of gender dysphoria?

Those moments when he has

a brief genderlessness.

Narcissistic too, in a

self-protective way.

Wrapped up in his own self

and self-pursuits.

Protection from the unpleasant.

Is all this not evidence that

he's mentally unwell?

He stands before an Angel

and fantasizes a day or even

a moment when all this

is wiped away clean

and he feels completely whole.

This is what heaven must be.

Convicted, but proven innocent of his

dark personality and life.

Born again!

Christmas tunes

Christmas tunes

from summer concert bands

on green grass carpets

stir within my whetted eye

a tearful melancholy joy

though in the heat of warm July

more than in the cold

of a mid December day.

It's now I want to sing

deck the halls,

and call to all ye faithful,

or five golden rings,

when the tiger lilies bloom,

neath a sky lit with stars

around the yellow moon.

Not when these are overheard

in every shop and frenzied crowd.

It's now I sing O Come Emmanuel,

bring joy to the world,

and silver bells -

from honey suckle shower wells

to air us fragrantly

amid the climbing rose.

It's that first noel,

and to the little town

of Bethlehem I go

to seek a needed Savior,

and sleep in heavenly peace.

Sleep in heavenly peace.

Fourth of July

Fourth of July

fireworks glitter high

with patriotic songs

from o'er the Rushmore sky,

as a civil war of hate

tells all is not so well

and worse,

has made this nation hell.

People have lost control

of anger and of lust,

morality is whatever

you alone think just.

Sickness epidemic

haunts this weary globe

killing whosoever,

wherever it may probe.

Even less

God bless the USA

is seldom heard

though some so few will say.

Make America great again

is a slogan of disdain.

Flags are burned

and statues ruined

reason is all in vain.

There is no peace when tyranny

strides maddened in our land;

destruction, violence and death

is completely out of hand.

O spacious skies

O amber waves of grain

O purple mountains majesty

above the fruited plains.

America!

America!

Yet still we sing it free,

God shed his grace on Thee.

See His Hands

Be healed in Jesus' Name!

He is alive and loves us so

and walks among us still.

See his hands extend

to heal you now

Kneel before him, bow!

He speaks a word to you

a word to meet your name.

Where is there pain?

Where is there fear?

What sorrow do you bear?

You can heal me Lord Jesus!

Touch me now Lord, here!

Glory to God the Father

who loves us so indeed

that He heals and delivers

us from all sickness

of mind and body needs.

See His hands touching

you now

this very moment.

Spirit and Truth

Seek not your God in buildings,

I heard him say to me -

where routine smothers spirit

and heart is absent, see!

A time will come, already here

I heard him say to me -

when neither mont Jerusalem

true worship will there be.

Then every soul a temple,

I heard him say to me -

where my own Spirit dwells,

in life abundantly.

Seek not your God in many

I heard him say to me -

but in your room, a silence where,

my Father there speaks free.

We worship what we know,

I heard him say to me -

the Father in the Spirit,

in Truth most tenderly.

Pandemics have a season,

I heard him say to me -

indeed it has a reason,

ordained most purposely.

I drew you from each other,

I heard him say to me -

that you might seek within,

to worship properly.

Abandon now your many gods,

I heard him say to me -

stand instead with lifted hearts

and minds sincerely.

I'm tired of your substitutes,

I heard him say to me -

your vacant voice and worthless words,

performed, repeated ritua'ly.

My Father seeks your spirit-hearts,

I heard him say to me -

My Father is a Spirit,

true worship, spiritually.

I therefore urge you brothers, sisters;

I heard him say to me -

offer yourself a living loss,

pleasing God wholly.

True and proper worship,

I heard him say to me -

transforms, renews your mind;

his perfect will you'll see.

True worshipers I seek,

I heard him say to me -

like you who heed my words,

and love wholeheartedly.

Yes, come together people

I heard him say to me -

Come and care and love each other,

a new commandment be.

I was asked

I was asked why so many people leave the Catholic Church? I think there are many reasons and they are often peculiar to each person. But I think there is a primary reason. The primary reason is rather clear it seems to me. It has to do with experience.

The Catholic Church does not offer a vital spiritual life experience to the average person, though some take hold of it anyway. That's why it has so many average lukewarm Catholics. Most often it offers a religion of repetitive traditional ritual with bells and incense. What's needed is a heart-felt and personal relationship to the Father, to Jesus and the Holy Spirit which makes the Christian faith alive and fervent, and results in a faithful and vital commitment.

Without this, all you have is religious repetition and ritual - which though often meaningful and beautiful - does not in itself sustain and grow one's faith and spiritual life or sustain one's commitment.

The experience of the eternal life of God within is essential. Eternal life is knowing the Father and Jesus Christ whom He has sent. The Catholic Mass for instance, which is the center of Catholic faith experienced week after week, is a meaningful ritual; but for most people it is not a spiritually fulfilling experience. The Catholic Sunday service must be changed radically in order for it to be vitally experienced rather than just witnessed.

The focus of Catholic education must become more experiential and personal. From an early age children must be personally fed with a felt experiential relationship to the living Father, Jesus, and Holy Spirit.

123

Too often Catholics have been fed an attractive variety of rich peripherals and not what is most essential. The beauty and richness of Catholicism has often masked the essential need for a personal relationship with God. The Church has either bored people to death or cluttered their lives with so much that the Lord has been lost in the excess and cannot be experientially discovered.

The church you never leave is the one within where the Trinity dwells.

Martyr

I am a nun.

I swish about doing good

with a perpetual smile

upon my face.

I have such high ideals

in this pagan land,

seeing Christ in everyone.

But don't need Mary mother

like I disavowed my own

and needed father more,

made me a lesbian.

I am raped by terrorists

who don't know a nun

but only see a woman

with a smile

who is vulnerable.

I cry out to God

but the ugly, sweaty

ape ejaculates in me.

I am so worthless now

so he kills me,

and I am glad to die.

It's always the same when

evil meets good.

Always a crucifixion.

In an instant

I reach beyond the confines of

my finite nature to embrace

the infinite being called God,

not after a long life of

striving after holiness

and doing good,

but from one evil act of violence

I enter heaven.

Dark Night

Now come with me into the cave

no sun or moon or light;

walk tenderly and stumble must

all unknown a fright.

Hold my hand though it's not there

and slowly follow me;

though you are blind

look deep, though nothing can you see.

Strip down to ugly nakedness

where my delight does shine;

hold fast to nothing carefully

for you alone are mine.

Throw off all sweet religion

the sacred pageantry;

forsake the hymns and sounds

of ceremony.

For now's the time

tis now the season

to take from you

both faith and your proud reason.

All faith and trust and love

you doubt have meaning now,

you've lost your faith you say?

Or purer it's somehow?

Your safe and solid edifice

has tumbled down, is past;

now all is gone but Me alone

to hold and cherish fast.

Distaste for what has gone before

is vomit in your soul

a purer drink and richer food

but yet you must behold -

Tis dark, so dark,

a dark night's spirit walk;

a blindness sees, a deafness hears,

without a light or talk.

Come away with me this night

into a desert place,

where only in the Spirit-wind

your closeness you can trace.

O death worth dying

bereft of all but Me,

now you can't touch

now you can't see.

Free! At last you're free!

Goin' Home

Our souls returning home

the story of our life;

and though the journey long

and lost at times

we still will travel on.

The soul is always forward bent

the next step it pursues,

it knows where is its home -

there is no turning back.

So the Isrealites left Egypt

and Odysseus,

or the Prodigal to his home?

The Pilgrim's Progress or

the Story of a Soul,

and the Confessions

of Saint Augustine?

We all are going home.

Goin' home! Goin' home!

I'm just goin' home.

Pilgrimage

Our pilgrimage was first begun

Before creation made its run;

For God had you and me in mind

Before there was created time.

In Romans eight, verse twenty-nine

God had us clearly in his mind.

He formed our image very new,

For there it says He us 'foreknew'.

He also formed for us a plan,

So long before we came on land;

Before the sky or earth or sea,

it says that He 'predestined' me.

Enveloping

He is a stream of purest water flowing.

I sometimes step into it with bare feet

on a hot summer day, and I am refreshed.

He is snow and ice on my patio.
He gives me chills if I dare bare myself to it.

He is a swift waterfall which carries me along

and drops me into a deep pool of unknowing.

All about me and in me now, but I do not drown.

I say I must pray because it is a new day;

because it is sunrise. But it's not a new day for Him.

She is always there with swollen breasts

caring for her young.

There are no sunrises and sunsets for Him.

There are no new days, only one

continuous *now* that always was and is and will be.

So I must step into the *Now,* now.

Do I pray to Him during my waking hours?

Do I attempt to arouse His attention?

There are no hours or sleeping.

He is wide awake.

I cannot escape his gaze.

He is awe full.

Zeitgeist

Breathe it in and out

that toxic air about

a hostile hatred shout

abolish Christian clout

Punish and provoke

no this is not a joke

hate all Christian folk

let not the Word be spoke

Arrest, remove them all

if need be with a brawl

create a numbing pall

blaspheming every call

No gospel shall be heard

the Bible must be blurred

secular ways preferred

truth must be reword

Control the media now

whatever way, somehow

to pagan gods we bow

this is the cherished tao

Power and violence

destroy the innocence

no holy nonsense

from morals abstinence

The spirit of this age

is once again the rage

the devil is backstage

controlling this outrage

The thinking of this time

is like a hidden slime

which spreads to every clime

the newest paradigm

O Christians speak the more

this is the surest cure

awake the dead, restore

the truth again once more,

the truth

again

once more.

Renew

(A slow word-by-word prayer-meditation)

One Jesus, to you I must return;

lead me to the Father Two,

and by your precious Spirit Three,

in me, renew.

ONE JESUS (praise the name)

TO YOU (only you)

I (my name, You know me very personally; Ps 139)

MUST (a necessity, can't live otherwise)

RETURN (where have I been? Is 53:6)

LEAD ME (I need your help)

TO THE FATHER (my Abba, dear Abba; almighty God)

TWO (He and Jesus make two one)

AND BY YOUR (Jesus' own Spirit; Rom 8:9)
PRECIOUS SPIRIT (Active Holy Spirit in my spirit, Rom 8:11)

THREE (The Blessed Trinity)

IN ME (they dwell and are alive in me)

Sylvia

Sylvia Plath is a haunting name to me,

not only because she ended her own life by suicide

but because she was like every intense and talented person

who is also tormented and troubled.

She could never reconcile her two selves, the yellow and white of her.

She was schizophrenic and bipolar, but remember, brilliant, lonely.

I can feel for her, with her. And so am attracted to her as person and
poet.

Without, inhibited, restrained; within explosive with emotion.

She wrote slowly with her hand-held dictionary and thesaurus

looking for just the right word or creating conflict and confusion

like she was inside when she let herself go impulsively

and scrambled words and spaces, and made nonsense except to herself

and to those who know how to read good poets.

Genius erupted from her chaotic, violent, raging placidity.

Caught in her Bell Jar under extreme pressure vacuum emptiness.

Tedium and depression suffocated.

She crawled under the fruit cellar with a bottle of sleeping pills,

found by her brother after several days half-dead.

While people heaped praise on her, she felt even more worthless.

But she couldn't stop writing.

Then raped by professor Irwin.

Psychiatric recovery took awhile.

Anguish vented on her typewriter.

Ariel sums it up well but obscurely.

Graduated summa cum laude with a Fullbright to Cambridge.

Her suicide some years later, after marriage and children,

inhaling gas from an oven, provokes wonder and mystery.

Some people like Sylvia are so complex with tormented minds

and talented spirits, that life is just too much for them,

and at some point it all comes crashing down,

unbalanced and unmanageable, the inner demon voice

becomes more convincing than the loving voice of God.

(from *A Closer Look at Ariel*

by Nancy Hunter Steiner)

Night

I went to catch the early dawn

when all is still around;

when air is clear, I captured scents,

faint morning birds their sound.

As Emerson I hoped to be

alone with nature's god;

left all alone my cabin home

where native settlers trod.

Run fast while there's still night

plead not for prolonged sleep;

so swift the heavens pass away

neglecting nightfall's starry deep.

Recline upon the bosom earth

gather diamonds slowly passing;

see the marble shining orb,

listen for the axis pole soft spinning;

gaze into the dark expanse above,

and count the ways I love - you.

Prophecy One

I saw a crumbling church

around me lay the ruins

debris before my feet

no entrance to ascend

I tried to climb within

but was not able to

a mighty hand held me

said do not enter in

I am not there

no longer here

I have been long cast out

they knew me not

they prayed in lies

just mirrors all about

I tore them down

all to the ground

their useless monuments

I ran away

and hid from them

so they would have to seek

no ritual and panoplies

they spit out week to week

now and evermore

I have abandoned them

until they rend their hearts

and cry and weep

I will no longer be

convenient god adored

with fluffy words

and angry swords

I am so broken-bored

Away with you

you theater devotee

you paid your entrance fee

why are you here

what masks you wear

what did you come to see?

I never knew you

my supposed friends

your voice to me was numb

you drank and ate

and festivaled

and left me only crumbs

Search for me and seek me

until I find the ones

who real, pure loves

me with whole-heart

then I will come to him

and dwell within

and from him never part.

SARX

The Holy Spirit is a divine Person of the Trinity God. O, so forgotten, unknown. A real Person; wholly Spirit, loving, life-giving, chasing after me and you with beams of radient tenderness. He is the emissary of the Father and Jesus.

We call him the *Holy* Spirit because he is the Spirit of holiness, goodness, joy and love. O Loving Spirit Person, wherever you begin to work in a person's life, you dispel spiritual darkness, you bring light to spiritual truth, you convict us of sin and evil, and give new spiritual life by showing us the goodness of the Father and Jesus Christ.

When yout fall upon a community, revival breaks out; unbelievers and lukewarm nominal Christians receive new spiritual births. When you, Holy Spirit of the Father and Jesus enter our lives, we have a new boldness to witness and proclaim the good news of Jesus Christ, we see signs and wonders of your miraculoous action in mental and physical healing, deliverance from evil, conversions, changed lives and new hope.

You give us a new power in prayer and a power to overcome sinful habits. In fact, all that we saw when Jesus ministered on earth, we see happen when you begin your work. The only difference is that Jesus, filled with you Holy Spirit, did these wonderful things himself; but now most holy Spirit you work through and in us.

You said to me: This present time is a time of God's judgment. you can feel it in the air. You can see it in the restlessness, unhappiness, and searching taking place in people's lives. You can see it in the way evil and sin have escalated everywhere. As in the time of Moses, people dance around the golden calf - let me list them boldly - immorality, impurity, sensuality, greed, crime, hatred, fighting, strife, apostasy, idolatry, orgies, drunkenness, sexual offenses, child abductions, child sexual abuse, women sold into prostitution,

143

unprecedented indulgence in sin, and addictions of all kinds. Sinful practices and perversions are engaged in without restraint or shame. Nations against nations. Political crises one after another. The creation of more deadly nuclear weapons. Uncontrolled environmental change and epidemics to come. The world is out of control and lost without the Father and Son. Churches have collapsed. People have lost their faith. Many of the shepherds themselves have broken trust with the sheep. The world is without a Shepherd. Christ may return soon, but if not - then there surely will be an outpouring of my Spirit, says the Lord.

He reminded me os a spiritual saint, pastor Blumhardt; who in a time of great spiritual turmoil, said: *"let us pray and hope for a new outpouring of the Holy Spirit. It must come if the level of our Christian living is to change. We cannot go on in this miserable way. Those first powers and gifts (of the Holy Spirit given to the apostles) are meant to return, and I believe that our dear Lord is only waiting for us to desire them."*

Each of you must earnestly seek the outpouring of the Holy Spirit. Pray for spiritual awakening and renewal. Make it the prayerful desire of your heart that the Father once again release a wave of the Holy Spirit upon the people of God and the churches, and on those who sincerely desire a time of Pentecost.

The Holy Spirit comes to dwell in the believer in Christ. In John 14: Jesus says, *"If you love Me, keep My commandments. And I will pray the Father, and He will give you another Helper, that He may abide with you forever—the Spirit of truth, whom the world cannot receive, because it neither sees Him nor knows Him; but you know Him, for He dwells with you and will be in you. I will not leave you orphans; I will come to you."*

Let us pray that we not be left as orphans; without parents, for we are children of the Father, Son and Holy Spirit. Let us call upon our Father to release his Helper into our world, who is already in our hearts. Let us be born again by the Spirit, for the Spirit gives birth to spirit. *"The wind blows wherever it pleases. You hear its sound, but you cannot tell where it comes from or where it is going. So it is with everyone born of the Spirit.* " Father, let us hear the wind again! Let us feel his power stirring and renewing our churches and all Christians.

Notice again and again that Jesus says we show our love and loyalty to him by keeping his commandments and word. And when we do, the Holy Spirit is released with power in us.

Indwelling of the Father, Son and Spirit

In John 14: it also says, *"A little while longer and the world will see Me no more, but you will see Me. Because I live, you will live also. At that day you will know that I am in My Father, and you in Me, and I in you,"* (what else can this mean than that They will come to us spiritually, in the Spirit). *"He who has My commandments and keeps them, it is he who loves Me. And he who loves Me will be loved by My Father, and I will love him and manifest Myself to him."*

"Judas (not Iscariot) said to Him, "Lord, how is it that You will manifest Yourself to us, and not to the world?" Jesus answered and said to him, "If anyone loves Me, he will keep My word; and My Father will love him, and We will come to him and make Our home with him." (Again what else can this mean than that the Holy Trinity of divine Persons will come to us spiritually, in the Spirit).

This morning I heard the Spirit speak to me from Galatians five where Saint Paul speaks about about the war between the Spirit and the flesh. I knew this already but this time I heard the Spirit speak to me most personally. That's when the Word of God is like a two-edged sword, cutting deep into my understanding and convicting me of the Spirit's work in my heart. This was no delightful dove of peace but a *fire* of conviction, convincing and cleansing.

Let me explain first with a word about Paul's letter to the Galatians. Paul became enraged when he discovered that some Jews were saying that Christians needed to be circumcised to fulfill the law. No, said Paul. Now we are free of the ritual laws that once burdened and obsessed him. There was a time when he was sure God was very pleased with him because he was a very good Pharisee, observing and obeying every letter of the law. But no longer. He saw how hollow a

145

relationship to God he had when he tried to justify himself by obeying the laws. The law did not nurture a relationship with the Father. Righteousness is not a legalistic perfection but only is in Christ. In faith and love. All the law is fulfilled in the love of God and neighbor. He understood that Christ had called him to preach the gospel of salvation based on faith and grace, not on the law.

Verses sixteen through twenty-two of this fourteenth chapter of John are most important. It is especially in these verses that I heard the personal voice of the Spirit speaking to me. Here he confronts the true reality of life which Christ taught us. Life is a war between the Spirit and the flesh (sarx) within us. Sarx is the Greek word for body or flesh, but not here in Galatians. Here the flesh means the sinful self, the old human nature which tries to save himself by the works of the law. But the flesh cannot overcome sin without the indwelling Holy Spirit because it is weak; so very, very weak.

Here in Galatians he tells us that the Spirit and the sinful self are opposed to each other. To defeat the sinful self we must walk by the Spirit; that is, we must try to surrender or yield to the promptings and voice of the Holy Spirit continually. Let the Spirit have power over us and empower us. As for me, I know when I do yield and when I don't yield to the Holy Spirit. When I don't yield I see the works of the flesh in my life. *"Sexual immorality, impurity and debauchery; idolatry and witchcraft; hatred, discord, jealousy, fits of rage, selfish ambition, dissensions, factions and envy; drunkenness, orgies, and the like."*

When I do yield to the Spirit, I see his fruit in my life: *"But the fruit of the Spirit is love, joy, peace, patience, kindness, goodness, faithfulness, humility and self-control."* My life and relationship to the Father, to Jesus and to people is so much better when these fruit are operating in my life. They are the signs of the authentic Christian follower of Christ.

"I will pour water on the thirsty land and streams on the dry ground; I will pour out my Spirit on your offspring and my blessing on your descendants, so that they will spring up like grass in a meadow, like poplar trees by flowing streams." **Isaiah 44:1-2.**

CLOUD

A russet breasted robin

darts across the morning lawn

three-stepping

in-and-out the bright green

and lightless shadows;

even so I footfall

across the heart of God,

both light and dark.

No knowing Him

seek him as i might

he draws me by a thread

to a distant height

where nothing do I know

only love is all i do

in quiet desired gasps

or sometimes breathlessly;

struck speechless dumb

worthless words keep silent

in the cloud of unknowing.

Run swiftly, collect some honey

before severely stung!

Love and leave quickly

less i suffocate

by his consuming love;

small bites of his flesh

small sips of his blood

a particle of bread

a drop of wine only

can i endure

less faint and my shuddered soul

evaporates into his abyss,

and i weep,

sweet weeping.

Fans and Followers

Consider how unusual

is your version and practice

of Christianity as may appear to others.

How strange and bizarre it may seem.

Looked at my own through an outsiders eyes

and was surprised

how unattractive or even repulsive

it may appear.

And I know when I look at others

I am ashamed and even angered

by some portrayals of Christian faith.

Preachers outrageously offensive,

and naive people contributing such money

to these charlatans

who become wealthy beyond imagination.

Abusers of the littlest sheep,

the innocents so loved.

Exploitation in the name of Christ.

To hell, to hell!

Where is the true faith and church of Christ?

Where is authentic Christianity to be found?

Jesus has a lot of fans, but few followers.

Ephesians 2

Through Christ Jesus

I [your name] have access [admittance; entrance]

to the **Father**

by the Spirit.

In Christ Jesus

I [your name] have become

a *dwelling* [temple; home]

in which

God the Father

lives

by his Spirit. [the Spirit of Jesus]

I am a Nest

Christ lives in me

I have become a nest

for Christ and the Father;

watched over, nurtured, grown,

by the Holy Spirit.

Easy Christianity

If I don't have to believe in God,

Do I?

When all the reasons for which I have

been Christian slipped away one day:

my Christian upbringing,

my Christian

family, friends, church,

ways of praying, routines;

the Christian culture that

has always been there

and assumed -

I cease belief in Christ.

I gave it up -

or maybe had to go deeper.

I've led a Christian life

without a sacrifice.

Guard your heart with your head,

not the other way around!

Has my faith been simply beneficial

or is it really true?

God, you mess with me sometimes

to test me by your love.

You pull from under me the rug

to make me build on rock.

Take all away in all the world

so I might find the truth.

Like Job I am strip-clean

and ask where have I been?

Does truth exceed what I believed,

encompass even more

than what I held so dearly

kept safely from my door?

Is this your tough refining

rather than black or white.

Go deeper says the Master

than what you thought just right.

I hear you kept commandments,

that is well and good,

but now I ask you give away,

come follow me you should.

I'll have no place to rest my head,

no den I can call home.

They'll rail at me

and cut me to the bone.

Easy Christianity

was comfortable and nice.

I never wondered is it true,

its comfort did suffice.

You messed me up on purpose,

you left me all alone;

to fall apart, discard,

and question what I've known.

I never really knew you

until you cut me deep.

I was at home with faith

so pleasant and so cheap.

Problems are not problems,

problems are transitions.

They shout a big alarm:

you're stuck and standing still,

you must see the harm.

I'll call you Straight-jacket Joe

from head to toe

instead of Spirit and life.

Break down!

Break out!

Break through!

then shout: I've found

the way, the truth, the life.

Il Poverello

I see the wrecked remains,

undomed, the broken fallen walls,

stones all scattered 'bout;

the marred mucked cross

brought me to tears,

and stirred an anxious doubt.

The tower's bell

swung loose and frail

within the steepled peak;

a breezy touch from

heav'ns breath

tolled softly with a sweak.

I knelt with heavy heart

to hear a word from God,

a whisper soft and clear;

welled up imploring me,

rebuild my church!

Start here!

Stone by stone I labored,

at first I was alone,

then others came along;

laughter brought the Spirit,

humor eased the work,

the walls grew with a song.

These sunny days

drew crowds

from hamlets all around;

our little band

of workmen looked just like

some foolish clowns.

The restoration

then complete

with joyful celebration

we thought our work was done.

Not so, he said,

it has just begun.

Awaken her!

Go raise the dead!

My Spirit's sweeping through.

Dead bones together gather,

old life's giv'n new.

My people languish

for shepherds sleep

or lead my lambs away.

I myself will call them;

those who've gone astray.

I'll pound their hearts,

unlock their ears

and singe their eyes with fire,

till spirits shake

and I remake

my children to expire

with love for me

and for my Son,

to dwell in trinity.

What is God?

What is God?

That's what I said,

you heard it right.

I'm asking What, not Who.

That word "God"!

Does it mean anything anymore?

Did it ever mean anything?

A childhood leftover of ages past,

an explanation for natural phenomenon,

a projection of wishful thinking,

a provision for human ignorance

an appeasement for the fear of death?

I and God have been connected

since I was seven years old.

For most of my life

God was down the street

and around every corner.

God was the long walk to church

when I altared boy.

God was always around

in one way or another.

The small statue on the bureau

with the votive light,

the crucifix on the wall.

I had no idea what or who God was.

I lived in a religious haze-maze.

Religion, but not God.

Ignorance of God.

Then I heard a beating drum

resounding in my soul,

getting louder, louder, louder.

I clung to God the more.

Matters not if you're

an intransigent atheist or sincere believer.

I don't care.

It's still a valid question.

Must be pondered sooner or later.

It's existence has much to do

with What it is.

No existence without essence.

What is the substance of God?

Pooffff!

OK, so Otto called it:

"Mysterium tremendum et fasciens."

The fearful and fascinating

incomprehensible, overwhelming mystery.

Attractive, seductive, satisfying,

transcendent, elusive, unverifiable, inaccessable.

I love the word "mystery".

That God is mystery takes hold of me

and satisfies me. I can take hold

of God the Mystery.

I can tolerate a mystery.

Mystery is a thing I can grasp

because, while unknown, I know it's there.

Mystery makes me wonder.

Wonder is exciting.

I can live with God as mystery.

When I ask *Who* God is,

I know it's rooted in both

my personal and social experiences.

I can answer that. It's about religion!

Religion is how I relate to God.

Religion is about Who God is.

Christians say God is Father, Jesus, Holy Spirit.

Muslims say God is Allah.

Jews say God is Jehovah.

India and Japan have many "divines" or deities.

Native Indians say God is Nature.

Religion gives God names

and tells us how to relate to God

and how God relates to us.

Who God is, is based on experiences which

each of these cultures have with the mystery.

What does my experience tell me about God?

But religion is not What God is.

Theology is not God.

What God is, is what we think of as

that omnipresent divine Being of our universe

who created it all.

The Big Being out there somewhere

and perhaps everywhere.

God is a divine superBeing of

mystery, depth, beauty, goodness, truth, life and love.

These are basic life pursuits.

These derive from those things

we most desire. They suggest that

if there is a longing in me for these things,

in order to be

embraced, completed, perfected and fulfilled,

then there must be an

all-embracing, all-completing,

all perfecting, all-fulfilling Being

which I call God.

We figure out God from the thirst in us.

God makes its reality known by my

longing for these things.

We say that

God is the ultimate *Mystery* which intrigues us.

It is the ultimate solid ground

and *Depth* of all existing things.

It is the ultimate *Beauty* that appeals to us.

It is the great *Goodness* we desire.

It is the ultimate Light of what is *Truth*.

It is the highest principle and essence of *Life*.

It is the perfection of all *Love*.

I don't like calling God "It".

Suddenly a reverie!

God is the Silent One.

I must adapt to his silence.

He draws me into his eternal silence.

I meet him in silence.

God invites me into his silence,

and it is good to be here.

An endless vista of green fields

and Fuji snow-capped mountains.

Standing there alone,

Enveloped in his silence.

Unable to speak or move.

Only hear his wind winding

through my being;

my spirit strummed by his Spirit,

on holy ground.

I remove my shoes

and leave the world behind.

Spirit to spirit communion.

Simply be on him in spirit.

I become invisible and silent like him

leaving this world for an eternal moment.

I conclude that I need him.

So I search here and there.

Salt Lake City, Rome, Bombay, Tokyo,

London, Mexico, Uganda, Iran.

I must find him

to be completed, perfected and fulfilled.

Yet this cannot be accomplished in one mortal life.

Then my eyes were opened and

I recognized him

in the light of the gospel

showing the glory of Christ

who is the image of God.

Food

On the grassy slopes of Galilee

his Son sat down to rest,

Five thousand men and more came by,

seeking to be blest.

This man is a healer,

he makes the sick souls well,

He gives to us the Father's life,

that He in us might dwell.

He preached to them the Word of God

until their souls were filled,

At supper time there was no food,

five barley breads, two fishes grilled.

This man is a healer,

he makes the sick souls well,

He gives to us the Father's life,

that He in us might dwell.

The disciples sat the people down,

as this man asked them to;

He prayed and gave the Father thanks,

as he would have us do.

This man is a healer,

he makes the sick souls well,

He gives to us the Father's life,

that He in us might dwell.

Twas then that from his blessed hand

the bread and fish rushed out.

Everyone was satisfied

as Jesus walked about.

This man is provider,

he makes the hungry full,

He gives to us the Father's life,

that He in us might dwell.

O Jesus feed us with yourself,

we are hungry still.

Satisfy this thirst in me,

and with yourself fulfill.

Chaos

I'm seeing all things clearly now.

I see through time to what will be.

I speak in prophecy,

declare and firm avow.

I'm seeing that some end is near,

with torments all about;

begun with frenzied shouts,

destroying much that's dear.

All the laws of nature scorned,

all courtesies despised;

the fam'ly flauntingly revised

and life itself so widespread torn.

People caught in freaky myths

which comfort, reassure.

Hiding eyes a hazy blur,

erecting some new monolith.

Apparitions everywhere

and prophecies galore;

predictions of less or more,

and end times here and there.

The cracks are showing in the land,

the fissures in the fields;

the earth restrains its harvest yield,

and saplings turn to sand.

The social fabric torn ashred,

and civil wars abound.

Violence is all around,

anarchy and chaos spreads.

Judgment

Rainbows clapping at the sun

before a swaying sign of sins,

he stood amid the youthful crowd

Repent! Believe! Be born again!

Some listened, anger brewing

or answered, hatred spewing.

Costumed, masked, facades,

judge not, but love, each one

my Father's child.

Look deep these souls within

with Jesus' eyes and see

poor wretched ones,

young muddled sons

and daughters passion bound

trapped in troubled troughs.

Like little lost lambs

from cradles not late

already snatched and served

for the devil's plate.

Seeds, weak seeds

remembered past planted

sprout among the weeds.

Now the time of judgment

driving out the prince of earth.

Now the time of verdict

for their loving darkness deeds,

the Light pierce dimly

but then the brightness

of the Son.

Comfortably Numb

This generation cannot

silence endure,

nor can the God of silence

them allure.

From solitude they refrain,

nor can he defeat

their sad disdain.

Diversion, intensity;

to these they run

as ersatz for

single-minded intimacy.

Worship me with drumming

sounds and louder voices abound,

I cannot hear their hearts.

Having lost all sensitivity,

given over to sensuality

and crude impurity

His Spirit cannot be heard,

nor can he plant a quiet word;

their mind is busy dreaming

of pleasure plans they're scheming.

His loving wrath is now revealed,

which once was kindly sealed.

We give not glory or give thanks

though we say we know of him

but do not know him.

The wise become fools

exchanging images for him.

The foolish become his choice

as little trusting kids.

But fools keep thirsting,

salted waters drink devour

to assuage their thirst they think

but only thirsting more.

July/26/20/10AM

Today, this day, deserves a poem,

to capture this one perfect day,

no better in the year.

Never let it go, save it,

and tuck it away

in a drawer like potpourri

in a sack, then take it out

when I need a perfect day,

.

Air so pure, the flowers exhale

sending gentle aromas sweet;

and somewhere cooking

roasted peppers and sausage meat.

The panoramic sight of green,

in trees, in grass, bushes, plants,

I want to save them in my heart

when winter comes with icy rant.

A distant plane hums in the sky

and cars pass by unseen

infrequently, for it is Sunday

in a quarantine.

The vibrant sunlight painted

on the lawn, and shadows

where the sunlight's gone.

And Oh, the breeze, the lusty breeze

seducing my arms and legs and face,

a perfect blend of cool and warm

gives no offense.

Sitting in the sun, leaning in a chair,

away from everyone.

Soaking vitamin D, wishing I too were green

in nature's panoply.

The tiny wrens delight my ear

with busy babies nesting

in the garden birdhouse near.

White butterflies disappear

in the queen Ann's lace,

chipmunks running in a kind of race.

And thanking Him for such a life,

protected and provided so

by love and grace and goodness; Oh,

the Spirit One who in my heart I know.

O yes, today, this perfect day

deserves a poem, so it not pass away.

LIMERICK CONTEST

1.

When Louisa was told by her mother

to watch over her two-year old brother,

the hydrant went on,

and made such a pond,

that he nearly went down in the gutter.

2.

Little Lulu was told by her mudder

to watch baby Bobby her brudder;

when the hydrant let go

it made such a flow

that Bobby slid down in the gudder.

3.

Little Lulu was watching her brother

who at first was quite calm in the gutter;

when the hydrant discharged

and the water enlarged,

her brother cried out for his mother.

4.

Alice was asked by her mother

to cool off her new baby brother;

so she brought him outside

and gave him a ride;

but he cried in the slide of the gutter.

5.

Maria was asked by her mother

to cool off her new baby brother;

so she brought him outside

and gave him a ride;

but he cried by the side of the gutter.

WHO DO I LISTEN TO?

Heretics, charlatans,

false teachers,

tired preachers galore.

The Christian landscape

is crowded with media

masters preying on

the uninformed and needy.

Ah, but a day is coming when

they all will be wiped

from the TV screens.

They have misled, deceived,

and devoured

the children of God.

Oh, where are the truth tellers?

Where are the true teachers?

Who do I listen to?

Who do I follow?

Who speaks the Word of God

or talks about Sin

Salvation

Repentance

Satan

Sanctity

Holy Spirit

Baptism

Body and Blood

Kingdom

Forgiveness

Service

Sacrifice

Born Again

Father

Jesus

Faith

Trust

Mercy

Love

Prayer

Praise

Thankfulness

Fruit

Gifts.

Jesus spoke these words.

Listen to Him!

He will I follow!

AMOS

When Amos opened his mouth

the voice of God came out,

but they did not know it was

the Lord who spoke.

"For three sins, even for four,

I will not back off," Amos said.

"When the ram's horn blows a warning,
shouldn't the people be alarmed?
Does disaster come to a city
unless the Lord has warned his people?

Go ahead, keep offering sacrifices to the idols.

They make not a sound.

They speak not a word,

nor do they give crops or heal you.

I brought hunger to every city
and famine to every town.

But still you would not return to me,

I struck with blight and mildew.

Locusts devoured all your fig and olive trees.

I sent illness on the people,

like the plagues I sent on Egypt long ago.

But still you would not return to me.

Prepare to meet your God in judgment.

Come back to me and live!

How you despise people who tell the truth!

Do what is good and run from evil

so that you may live!

There will be crying in all the public squares

and mourning in every street.

What sorrow awaits you who say,

'If only the day of the Lord were here!'

You have no idea what you are wishing for.

That day will bring darkness, not light.

In that day you will be like a man who runs from a lion—

only to meet a bear.

Escaping from the bear,

he leans his hand against a wall in his house—

and he's bitten by a snake.

I hate all your show and pretense—

the hypocrisy of your festivals and solemn assemblies.

I will not accept your burnt offerings.

I won't even notice all your choice peace offerings.

Away with your noisy hymns of praise!

I will not listen to the music of your harps.

Instead, I want to see a mighty flood of justice,

an endless river of righteous living.

The Sovereign Lord showed me a vision, said Amos.

I saw him preparing to send

a vast swarm of locusts over the land.

I saw him preparing to punish

his people with a great fire.

I will test my people with this plumb line.

I will no longer ignore all their sins.

"In that day," says the Sovereign Lord,

"I will make the sun go down at noon

and darken the earth while it is still day.

I will turn your celebrations into mourning

and your singing into weeping.

I will bring my exiled people

back from distant lands,

and they will rebuild their ruined cities

and live in them again.

They will plant vineyards and gardens;

they will eat their crops and drink their wine

The Lord has spoken,

and he will do these things.

MEETINGS

We complete our place and purpose

in a short lifetime.

This poet, this preacher.

A Jew, a Christian.

An atheist, a theist.

Each makes a contribution

to their own.

Each is praised and honored.

Both die the same year,

never knowing each other till now,

and what they have in common.

We read and listen to their legacy

with fond appreciation.

Words left behind.

Great-grandfathers both,

by generations to be remembered.

They live and watch and wait.

-:|:--:|:--:|:--:|:--:|:--:|:-

One sits behind bars for life,

another, the victim

lies in a grave at twenty-four.

They met in a convenience store

one night at closing

when a pistol shot sealed their bond.

-:|:--:|:--:|:--:|:--:|:--:|:-

This young adolescent boy

says heaven must be boring.

Trying to say death makes life

meaningless.

He questions his faith,

no longer a child.

-:|:--:|:--:|:--:|:--:|:--:|:-

An intellectually challenged boy

asks a similar girl to lunch;

awkward both.

Though attracted,

they say little to each other

but smile a lot.

She says she likes him.

He says he loves her.

She makes a card in their class

to say thank you.

Life feels wonderful.

They talk without making eye contact.

-:|:--:|:--:|:--:|:--:|:-

He wants to pray,

but only has desire;

no words emerge

for he is sleepy now, and must.

SUMMER JAR

The treetops sway,

a summer breeze;

yellow-white mirror-like leaves

rustling together in the wind,

reflect the sun rays,

high pitching a swish swish sound

like air pushed through an organ reed

prompts summer sadly passing

and angst of what's ahead.

Beholding onto each green blade

or uneaten leaf,

gathering tokens of summer;

sweet basil, tangy leaf tomato,

oregano, streamers of garlic chives,

in a jar, to put away

aromas for another day.

No life without the light.

I can a day's half endure in dark

to know the light will come;

but cloudy rainy winter days

I die without the Son;

who seeing, sees the Father,

makes me one.

BORN AGAIN

At night he came,

still the same,

attracted and enthralled

hoping to discover all

by this miracle-making man,

this life-changing preaching man.

Something was stirring deep within,

pulling irresistably to him;

then he heard him say

your religion is not the way,

You must be born again!

That's not what he desired to hear.

This he could hardly bear.

He came in confidence and pride,

and Jesus turned it all aside.

You must be born again!

He wasn't told how he was good,

but how he really stood

in the eyes of God on high

who loved him so and drew him nigh.

You must be born again!

He longed to hear that he was blesst,

was good, one of the very best.

But he was told that he was dead,

lost, deceived, bad, misled.

You must be born again!

You think that you can see,

but you are blind so woefully;

you think you are well informed,

it's not enough to be reformed;

You must be born again!

Self-confidence, pride were shattered,

his self-assurance sorely battered.

How can I crawl back in the womb,

I'm old and waiting for my tomb.

You must be born again!

Listen friend with inner ears,

it matters not your many years;

your spirit I am speaking of,

it must be born from God above.

You must be born again!

You ask me how that this can be,

and how God's kingdom you might see?

The Spirit moves, a silent wind,

he new life kindles deep within.

That's how you're born again!

Fall now upon your knees

and ask the Spirit as he please;

a new life born from God above

has filled you with his lavish love;

You now are born again!

Alleluia

Amen

www.ingramcontent.com/pod-product-compliance
Lightning Source LLC
Chambersburg PA
CBHW071941150726
47999CB00001B/278